The Big Orange Splot

Splot

by Daniel Manus Pinkwater

SCHOLASTIC INC.
New York Toronto London Auckland Sydney

For Estelle Schutz

ISBN 0-590-44510-3

Copyright © 1977 by Daniel Manus Pinkwater. All rights reserved. Published by Scholastic Inc.

20

1 2/0

Printed in the U.S.A.

23

Mr. Plumbean lived on a street where all the houses were the same.

3

He liked it that way. So did everybody else on Mr. Plumbean's street. "This is a neat street," they would say. Then one day . . .

A seagull flew over Mr. Plumbean's house. He was carrying a can of bright orange paint. (No one knows why.)

And he dropped the can (no one knows why)
right over Mr. Plumbean's house.

It made a big orange splot on Mr. Plumbean's house.

"Ooooh! Too bad!" everybody said. "Mr. Plumbean will have to paint his house again."

"I suppose I will," said Mr. Plumbean. But he didn't paint his house right away. He looked at the big orange splot for a long time; then he went about his business.

The neighbors got tired of seeing that big orange splot. Someone said, "Mr. Plumbean, we wish you'd get around to painting your house."

"O.K.," said Mr. Plumbean.

He got some blue paint and some white paint, and that night he got busy. He painted at night because it was cooler.

When the paint was gone, the roof was blue. The walls were white. And the big orange splot was still there.

Then he got some more paint. He got red paint, yellow paint, green paint, and purple paint.

In the morning the other people on the street came out of their houses. Their houses were all the same. But Mr. Plumbean's house was like a rainbow. It was like a jungle. It was like an explosion.

There was the big orange splot. And there were little orange splots. There were stripes. There were pictures of elephants and lions and pretty girls and steamshovels.

The people said, "Plumbean has popped his cork, flipped his wig, blown his stack, and dropped his stopper." They went away muttering.

That day Mr. Plumbean bought carpenter's tools. That night he built a tower on top of his roof, and he painted a clock on the tower.

The next day the people said, "Plumbean has gushed his mush, lost his marbles, and slipped his hawser." They decided they would pretend not to notice.

That very night Mr. Plumbean got a truck full of green things. He planted palm trees, baobabs, thorn bushes, onions, and frangipani. In the morning he bought a hammock and an alligator.

When the other people came out of their houses, they saw Mr. Plumbean swinging in a hammock between two palm trees. They saw an alligator lying in the grass. Mr. Plumbean was drinking lemonade.

"Plumbean has gone too far!"

"This used to be a neat street!"

"Plumbean, what have you done to your house?" the people shouted.

"My house is me and I am it. My house is where I like to be and it looks like all my dreams," Mr. Plumbean said.

The people went away. They asked the man who lived next door to Mr. Plumbean to go and have a talk with him. "Tell him that we all liked it here before he changed his house. Tell him that his house has to be the same as ours so we can have a neat street."

The man went to see Mr. Plumbean that evening. They sat under the palm trees drinking lemonade and talking all night long.

Early the next morning the man went out to get lumber and rope and nails and paint. When the people came out of their houses they saw a red and yellow ship next door to the house of Mr. Plumbean.

"What have you done to your house?" they shouted at the man.

"My house is me and I am it. My house is where I like to be and it looks like all my dreams," said the man, who had always loved ships.

"He's just like Plumbean!" the people said. "He's got bees in his bonnet, bats in his belfry, and knots in his noodle!"

Then, one by one, they went to see Mr. Plumbean, late at night. They would sit under the palm trees and drink lemonade and talk about their dreams — and whenever anybody visited Mr. Plumbean's house, the very next day that person would set about changing his own house to fit his dreams.

Whenever a stranger came to the street of Mr. Plumbean and his neighbors, the stranger would say, "This is not a neat street."

Then all the people would say, "Our street is us and we are it. Our street is where we like to be, and it looks like all our dreams."

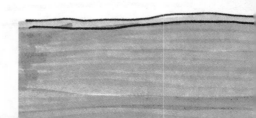